Peppa Pig™

The Tooth Fairy

Once upon a time there was a clever little pig called Peppa. She was very proud of her teeth.

Grunt! Grunt!

Peppa and her brother George knew how to take care of their teeth. Doctor Elephant, the dentist, had shown them. Peppa and George brushed their teeth every morning AND every evening!

Brush! Brush!

Peppa and George loved playing dentists.
Peppa would pretend to be Doctor Elephant
and George would be Miss Rabbit, her assistant.
George's toy dinosaur was the patient.
"What lovely clean teeth, Mr Dinosaur."
"PINK! PINK!" shouted George.
"Oh yes, Miss Rabbit, please give Mr Dinosaur
some pink medicine," said Peppa.

One day after playing their dentist game, Peppa and George were eating their tea. Suddenly, something fell onto Peppa's plate.

Clatter! Clatter!

It made Peppa JUMP!
"What's that?" she asked.
"Ho! Ho! It's a tooth," laughed Daddy Pig.
"But where's it from?" asked Peppa.

"Why don't you look in the mirror?" said Mummy Pig.
Peppa looked.
She had a BIG gap
in her teeth!
"Oh no!" she cried.
"Do we need
to go and see
Doctor Elephant?"
Peppa was very worried.

Ho! Ho! Ho!

"No," said Mummy Pig. "It's just a milk tooth. It's meant to fall out."

"A milk tooth? What's that?" asked Peppa.
"A milk tooth is a baby tooth," explained Mummy Pig.
"Oh!" said Peppa. "Will I grow a new one then?"
Mummy Pig nodded.

"What should I do with this milk tooth?" asked Peppa.
"If you leave it under your pillow tonight the tooth fairy will come.
She will take your tooth and leave you a shiny new coin in return!"
said Mummy Pig.

That evening, when Peppa watched television with her family, she kept thinking about the tooth fairy.

"When I grow up I want to be a tooth fairy!" said Peppa. Daddy Pig chuckled.

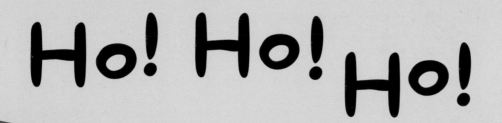

Ho! Ho! Ho!

"What about you, George?" asked Daddy.
George pointed at his dinosaur.
"Dine-Saw!" he growled.

Hee! Hee! Hee!

"Come on George," shouted Peppa,
"we don't want to miss the tooth fairy!"
They both ran up the stairs
to get ready for bed.
"Remember to clean your teeth!"
Mummy Pig called.

"What are you doing, Peppa?" asked Daddy Pig.
Peppa was carefully cleaning her tooth that had fallen out.
"I want my tooth to be nice and clean for the tooth fairy,"
said Peppa.

Snort!
Snort!

Hee!
Hee!
Hee!

Peppa put the tooth under her pillow.
"Are you sure the tooth fairy will be
able to find it?" she asked.
"I promise," said Mummy Pig.
"Just you wait and see!"

"Goodnight, Peppa and George!"
"Goodnight, Mummy! Goodnight,
Daddy! Grunt! Grunt! Hee! Hee! Hee!"

"I'm going to wait up for the tooth fairy," Peppa said.
"George! Let's not go to sleep."
George smiled and nodded.
Peppa waited, and waited . . .

Snore!
Snore!

She could hear something.
"Is that the tooth fairy?" wondered Peppa.
"George," she whispered, "can you see the tooth fairy?"
She peeped down at George. He was fast asleep.
It was him making the noise!

"I am much better at staying awake than George," sighed Peppa. She settled back on her bed with her eyes W-I-D-E open. After a while they started to close. Quickly she opened them again. "I am going to stay awake and see the tooth fairy," said Peppa firmly to herself.

Snore! Snore! Snore!

But soon Peppa was fast asleep!

Tinkle!
Tinkle!

What was that?

It was the tooth fairy!
"Hello, Peppa!" she whispered.
"Would you like a coin in
exchange for your tooth?"
She pushed the coin under
Peppa's pillow and pulled
out her tooth.
"What a lovely clean tooth,"
she said. "Thank you
very much!"

Flutter!
  Flutter!
    Flutter!

The next morning, as soon as Peppa opened her eyes, she leapt out of bed and looked under her pillow.
"Ooh! A shiny coin!" she shouted, jumping up and down with excitement. "Mummy, the tooth fairy did come after all!"
"I hope she thought my tooth was nice and clean," continued Peppa.

"Well, you certainly brushed it for long enough!" laughed Daddy Pig. "Oh, I wish I had seen the tooth fairy," sighed Peppa. "Next time, I'm definitely going to stay awake ALL night! Hee, hee, hee!"

Doctor Elephant's tips for nice healthy teeth

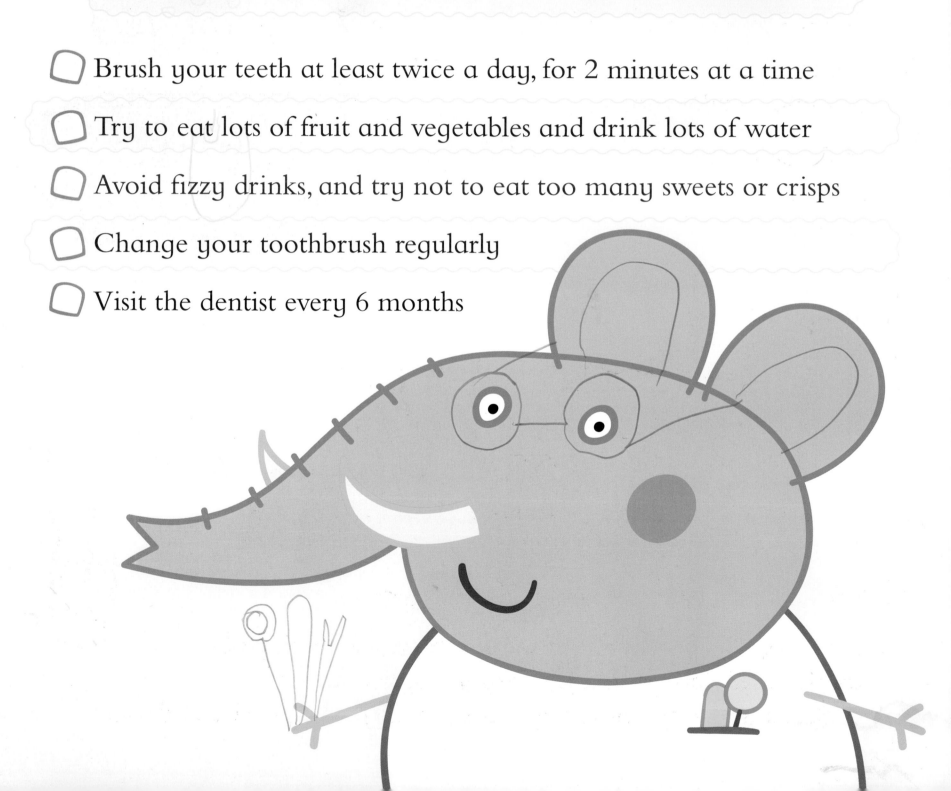

- [ ] Brush your teeth at least twice a day, for 2 minutes at a time

- [ ] Try to eat lots of fruit and vegetables and drink lots of water

- [ ] Avoid fizzy drinks, and try not to eat too many sweets or crisps

- [ ] Change your toothbrush regularly

- [ ] Visit the dentist every 6 months

How to brush your teeth:

Peppa

- ☐ Put a pea-sized blob of fluoride toothpaste onto your toothbrush

- ☐ Clean each tooth with a gentle circular motion

- ☐ Make sure you clean the whole surface of each tooth and clean right up to the gum line

Going to the dentist:

- ☐ Ask an adult to take you to the dentist to see what it's like

- ☐ Try playing in the waiting room if you don't want to see the dentist at first

- ☐ Sometimes dentists have stickers and colouring pages!

When your milk teeth fall out:

Don't worry! Keep your tooth safe, it's time for a visit from the tooth fairy! Soon you'll grow some big teeth.
Fill in the chart on the next page as each of your milk teeth fall out.

Tooth Chart

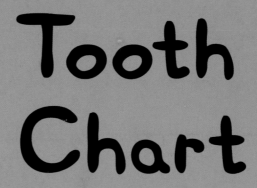

Upper

Left   Right

Lower

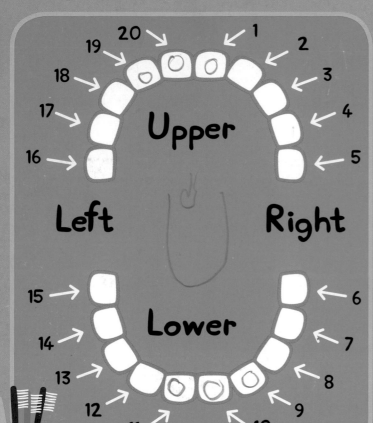

Tooth	Date it fell out	Tooth	Date it fell out
1 ✓		11 ✓	12·2·15
2 ✓		12 ✓	13·8·15
3		13	
4		14	
5		15	
6		16	
7		17	
8		18	
9 ✓	18·10·12	19 ✓	18·7·13
10		20 ✓	18·6·14